# Elspeth

## A Goldilocks Story in Three Acts

Jeff Gatlin

Laurelwood Press

*This is a work of fiction. Names, characters, places, and incidents are either the product of the author's imagination or are used fictitiously. Any resemblance to actual persons, living or dead, events, or locales is entirely coincidental.*

*The historical settings, geography, and cultural contexts depicted in this work are rendered as accurately as the author's research permits, but the characters and their stories are invented.*



Laurelwood Press

Hernando, Mississippi

# Contents

## GENEALOGY

*Deep into that darkness peering, long I stood there, wondering, fearing, doubting, dreaming dreams no mortal ever dared to dream before.*
— Edgar Allan Poe, "The Raven"

I am an amateur genealogist, which is to say I am a man who spends too many lunch hours and evenings in front of a screen following surnames through ship manifests and census records and county courthouse filings, chasing the dead through their paperwork. I have been doing this for over thirty years. The dead are not particularly interested in being found, but they leave trails anyway — in the records they filed and the taxes they paid and the children they registered and the land they deeded and the graves they were put into, if anyone thought to mark the graves, which not everyone did. The trail is always there. You learn to read it.

I have traced my own family back to circumstances some would rather I not have found — a part of American history that a genealogist encounters when he digs deep enough, the two columns on the same page of the same ledger, the name distributed like property to the people who were property. I have traced other families connected to mine by that history, following threads I had no obligation to follow but could not leave alone. That is the nature of the work. You pull a thread. You follow it. You find out where it goes.

Several years ago, on a Tuesday evening in the fall, I was sitting on the fourth floor of the Benjamin Hooks Central Library in Memphis — the genealogy section, the one that smells of old paper and microfilm, and has the particular stillness of a room where people come to find things they are not always prepared to find. I was there for my own reasons, following my own thread, when I found something I was not looking for and have not been able to put down since.

The library sits on Poplar Avenue, around the corner from Tillman Street in the Binghamton neighborhood of Memphis. I had kept offices on Tillman Street for twenty years. I lived with my parents and sister at the eastern edge of Binghamton until I was five years old, when we moved southeast to the suburbs that were being built out of old farmland, the way suburbs were built all around Memphis in the 1970's. I do not remember Binghamton with any clarity. I remember that the neighbors kept birds in a cage. I remember the store at the end of the street.

I was perhaps a quarter mile from Tillman Street when I found the name.

The name was Bär. A Bavarian family name meaning bear — common enough in the German-speaking world, unremarkable in its origins. I found it in a church record from a village at the edge of the Bavarian Forest in the middle of the nineteenth century. A woodcutter's family. A wife. A son called Pip, whose given name was Björn — bear in the old Norse tongue, a doubling that someone in the family had intended as a blessing. The church record after that entry goes silent in the way records go silent when something has happened that the surviving community preferred not to document. Not absent. Silent. After decades of researching genealogy I have learned to read that silence as carefully as the words.

I sat at that table for a long time before I moved on. I should have moved on sooner. I should have left the thread where I found it. I did not.

The name crossed the Atlantic with the boy who survived. He came to Mississippi in the years before the war, anglicized Bär to Behr on arrival — same root, same sound in any mouth — and settled in Quitman County, in the flat cotton country of the Delta. His Old World dreams came to the New World and he must have made the most of them. What the records show is that the name Behr appears in Quitman County in two columns on the same plantation manifest — the column for the white landholder and the column for the people he held, both recorded under the same name. The master's name distributed like property to the people who were property.

After emancipation the two lines diverge. The white Behr line fades from the records by the turn of the century. The other line stays — the line that carries both the name and the blood of the German landholder, the way such lines did throughout the Delta, the master's name and the master's blood both distributed without his consent being required or his acknowledgment ever given. By Edmund's generation the family's mixed appearance reflected that history in the way that Quitman County insisted on noting — in deed records, in census columns, in the careful designations that the county used to keep track of such things. Edmund and Mabel paid those designations no attention. A man is not a census column.

Edmund Behr. Mabel Behr. Their son Bruno, called Gus. Sharecropping the same land their grandparents had worked under a different legal arrangement, on the Coldwater River in Quitman County, Mississippi, in the years of the Depression.

I found the name a third time in a Memphis phonebook. A man named Gus Baer — one more small orthographic adjustment, the same sound in any mouth — residing in the Binghamton neighborhood two blocks from Tillman Street. He had come up from the Delta on the Illinois Central, the way people came up in those years, following the Great Migration out of the cotton country. His son. His grandson Marcus. The line continuing, the name carrying forward, the bear at the center of it in every iteration.

Bär. Behr. Baer. Three spellings. One sound. One meaning. The animal that is large and patient and dangerous and very hard to stop once it has decided to move.

What I also found, attached to each of these families at the moment their records go quiet or strange, was a description. Not always written. Sometimes only preserved in the oral accounts of neighbors, in letters, in the marginal notations of clerks recording something they could not categorize. A girl. Fair-haired. A pale nondescript dress. Nothing in her face you could hold onto.

I am a practical man by inclination and by profession. I designed building systems for a living — the mechanical infrastructure that makes a building work, that keeps the air moving and the toilets flushing and the temperature where it needs to be for people to function safely inside. I spend my days thinking about load calculations and system redundancy and the ways things fail when they are not designed correctly. I am not a man who reaches for explanations that exceed the available evidence.

What I can say with confidence is that the name travels and the description travels with it, across an ocean and a century and a half and the full width of American history, and that I have not been able to find a rational account that encompasses all three occurrences.

What follows are three accounts reconstructed from the sources available to me — historical records, oral histories, a police report filed in Memphis that I obtained through a public records request and that I have not been able to stop thinking about since. I have written them as narrative because that is the form they seem to require. I have not invented the essential details. I have, in places, supplied the connective tissue that the surviving records leave out.

I do not know who or even what she is. I know what she does. I know the name she follows and the houses she finds and the quality of silence she leaves behind her. I know that in each account there is a child who survives — a boy, always, always the smallest one, always with a bear's name somewhere in his given name, though by the third generation nobody knows this and the knowing has been traveling in the name without anyone to carry it consciously. I know that in each account there is an old man on the margin who sees her and knows, or almost knows, and cannot stop what is coming. I know that in the most recent account the old man moves, but not in time. Not fast enough to save everyone. Fast enough to save the child. I do not know if that is progress. I think the child would have been left alone anyway.

I have a son. He has a wife. They have a child. I know what kind of house they keep — the boots by the door, the knife kept sharp. When the boy is older there will be the drawing on the refrigerator in his wobbly but loving hand. I know exactly what kind of house they keep, because I raised the man who keeps it.

I wrote this book anyway. Make of that what you will.

*—J.G.*

*Hernando, Mississippi*

# Act 1

## ELSPETH OF THE DUNKELWALD

### I.

She came out of the wood in the early afternoon, when the light was still good and the path back to wherever she had come from was easy to find. Her dress was clean. This was always the part people would later find most difficult to explain — the dress. Pale, neat at the collar, not a mark on it despite coming out of the Bavarian forest. Her hair caught the light as she walked, very fair, loose around her shoulders and bright as hammered gold in the afternoon. Her eyes were clear and she walked the way she always walked, without hurry, without looking behind her.

A charcoal-burner named Oskar saw her emerge from the tree line near the old mill road. He had no reason at the time to pay particular attention, and therefore did not. A girl coming out of the Dunkelwald in the afternoon. What he noticed was the hair. Golden, he would say later, "very bright in the slanted light" as he later recalled it, "Golden Locks." She nodded at him, the brief indifferent nod of someone who does not intend to be remembered, and then she was past him and into the village.

Oskar went back to his burn. The charcoal would not wait for his curiosity. He did not think about her again until three days later, when they found the Bär cottage, and by then the thinking served no purpose except to remind him of what he had not done.

By then, of course, it was too late to think about anything useful.

* * *

Now go back. Go back to the beginning, which is to say go back to the morning, which is to say go back before the light shifted, before Oskar saw her, before anything was finished.

Go back to where it starts.

It always starts the same way.

## II.

Henrik Bär rose before the light, the way he always did. Not because the day required it — the trip to the high meadow could have started at mid-morning without any loss — but because Henrik had been rising before the light since he was fourteen years old and the habit had outlasted the necessity the way habits do when they are tied to who a man believes himself to be. He was a man who rose before the light. He was a man who had his tools in order. He was a man who kept his accounts, who met his obligations, who did not complain about the cold.

The cottage was small and orderly in the way of places where order is not merely preference but moral conviction. His tools hung on the wall by the door in graduated sequence — drawknife, adze, two hatchets, the long saw — each one cleaned and set back after use. His boots stood beside the door. Beside his boots, smaller, Marta's. Beside Marta's, smaller still, Pip's — the toes worn through at the left foot, which Henrik had noticed and meant to address before the cold came.

He built up the fire and, while the water heated, he unfolded the letter he kept in the inside pocket of his work coat, the one he'd read so many times the creases were going soft at the folds. It was from his cousin Werner, who had gone to America eight years ago and now wrote from a place called Ohio with the satisfaction of a man who has survived his own gamble and found the winnings sufficient. The letter described land — flat and dark and rich in the way that Bavarian forest land was not, land you could work without fighting it. A man could be something different there. Something with more room in it.

Henrik had been saving for three years. Not fast enough. Every time the number in the tin box under the loose board reached a level that felt like progress, something happened. The axle on the oxcart. A bad winter. And Vogt.

Vogt was the Jägermeister — the forest official, twenty-eight years old, broad-shouldered, with the particular confidence of a man who has been given authority and has not yet learned the difference between being respected and being feared. He came to the Bär property on official business more often than the work required. He always found something. A board cut a fraction wide of the permitted dimension.

A charcoal burn that had encroached two meters beyond the licensed area. The findings were never large enough to threaten Henrik's livelihood directly. They were always large enough to cost something. The fines went into Vogt's ledger and out of Henrik's tin box, and the distance between the Bär family and the port at Hamburg or Bremerhaven grew by whatever Vogt had decided to charge this time.

Henrik did not have a legal remedy. The forest law was not written for men like him. He paid the fines and thanked Vogt for his thoroughness and sent him on his way and went back to work and added the amount to the running total he kept against the day they would be gone from this forest forever.

Hamburg, he thought, stoking the fire in the dark. Bremerhaven. A ship. Werner's flat land. He heard Marta moving upstairs. Then Pip's feet on the boards overhead — running already, already talking to himself, already committed to the day.

Soon, Henrik thought. He folded the letter back into his pocket. Soon.

## III.

Marta Bär needed those minutes between Henrik's rising and Pip's — the kitchen to herself, the fire already going, the particular quiet of a woman thinking through her day before the day began talking back at her.

She had the porridge going before Pip was down the loft ladder, flavored the way each of them liked it: Henrik's with salt and rendered fat, her own plain from the pot, Pip's with a little of the late-summer honey they kept in the high cabinet and doled out with the careful affection of a hausfrau who understands that small pleasures require management to stay pleasurable.

She kept the kitchen the way she kept everything — with an exacting neatness that was not vanity but competence. The cook's knife hung from its hook above the preparation board, long and narrow, the blade kept bright and the edge kept true. She sharpened it every week whether it needed it or not, the stone's long whisper under her hands while her mind worked through whatever needed working through. This morning it was working through Vogt.

He had come again on Thursday. The timber inspection, always the timber inspection, rule book and official manner and the slow walk around the stacks that found nothing wrong because there was nothing wrong. He had stood in her kitchen doorway for ten minutes afterward, talking about nothing that required ten minutes. She had given him water and answered his questions and sent him on his way with the cool, precise courtesy she had developed for exactly this purpose over the past year. It cost her something every time — a making-small of exactly the parts of herself she most valued, the directness and the competence. She paid that cost because the alternative was worse, and she had weighed the alternatives with the same clear attention she brought to everything.

Henrik knew. He watched her manage Vogt with a look in his eyes she recognized as helplessness wearing the face of patience. She loved him for the patience. She wished the helplessness were otherwise. But there was Werner's letter. There was the tin box. There was the future Henrik was building toward with the same deliberate neatness he brought to his tools and his permits and the graduated boots beside the door.

She heard Pip on the loft ladder and turned from the hearth. The boy deserved her whole face, not the fraction left over from thinking about Vogt. He arrived in the kitchen the way he always arrived — completely, committed, already deep in a report about the beetles.

## IV.

Pip Bär was seven years old and called Pip because his given name was Björn — the old Norse word for bear, same root as Bär, a doubling that Henrik's father had intended as a blessing and that had become simply the boy's name, shortened to Pip by the miller's younger children who couldn't yet manage the consonant and then by everyone else.

He had his mother's dark eyes and his father's deliberate quality — that way of attending to a thing completely before moving to the next thing. He knew the birds by their calls and the trees by their leaves or bark. He had been tracking a colony of beetles under the flat stone by the herb bed for two weeks with the patience of a natural scientist and the investment of a boy who has chosen something as his own.

After breakfast he retrieved his pocketknife from the shelf — the handle he had carved himself from an elk-bone blank, intending a bear but the skill had failed him and it had become a fish instead, clumsy and earnest and entirely his. He put it in his pocket and went to check on the colony.

The drawing he had made three months ago was still pinned above the hearth: three figures in charcoal on a piece of birch bark, round and earnest, slightly too large for their legs, standing in front of a house that was more square than the actual cottage but captured its essential character — the door in the center, the two windows flanking it, the feeling of something solid and inhabited. Marta had put it up without ceremony and it had been there long enough to become part of the room.

The morning of the meadow trip, Pip crouched over the flat stone and lifted it carefully and confirmed the colony was undisturbed. He found, on the back of his own hand, a smaller beetle — green-black in the morning light, iridescent, making its way across his knuckles with tremendous purpose. He held very still and watched it for a long time. Then he set it gently back under the stone and replaced the stone carefully and went inside to wash his hands.

They left mid-morning, the three of them — the berry basket, Henrik's long saw for the windfall he'd been meaning to clear. Marta had covered the porridge pots and banked the fire. Henrik was quiet on the path, thinking about Werner's letter. Pip walked between his parents and talked about beetles. Marta listened with the particular quality of a woman attending to two things at once and managing both.

The cottage stood in the morning light, the door shut, the banked fire breathing slow inside it. It would be empty for a few hours. It would not be the same cottage when they returned.

## V.

Her name was Elspeth. This is the only thing we know about her that she did not choose for the occasion, and even that certainty has limits.

She had been in the Dunkelwald for two days before she found the Bär cottage. Not wandering — she did not wander. She moved with a specific, unhurried intention through the birch and pine, reading the forest's information the way a woodsman reads it: the smoke-trail that meant a dwelling, the wheel-ruts that meant a working household, the quality of the cleared ground that told her someone here was careful and organized and trusted their world enough to leave their door unlocked. The cottage had announced itself to her in fragments. She had let it, because approaching in fragments was always better than approaching directly.

She did not look any particular age within a range an observer could have named. In repose she looked young, almost fragile. In motion she looked like someone who knew exactly where she was going.

Her hair was the thing everyone mentioned first, always, without exception, which she had known since she was old enough to understand that people mentioned it. Very fair, very bright, loose around her shoulders, the kind of hair that catches light and holds it, that seems to generate its own illumination. Golden locks. The phrase was inevitable. She had heard it her whole life. She did not think about her hair. She thought about other things.

Her face was the thing people could not describe afterward, because they were trying to describe the absence of something rather than the presence of something, and absence is difficult to render in words built for presence. There was nothing in it you could hold onto. No performance of feeling, no social signaling. She met your eyes the way a tool meets a problem — with the full attention of an instrument calibrated for exactly this purpose, assessing what it found, registering what was useful, setting aside what was not. People felt seen by her. It was not a comfortable feeling.

She had been this way since childhood. Not troubled. Not slow. Simply elsewhere — present in body, attending to something interior that nobody else could access. She did not perform normalcy. She approximated it when necessary, the way someone who has learned a language from the outside speaks it correctly but without the music.

She was not without feeling. She recognized a well-kept household for what it represented. She knew what the graduated boots by the door meant, knew what the drawing above the hearth meant. She let the knowing in, controlled, in a measured amount — enough to see clearly, not enough to matter. She had learned to calibrate this the way you calibrate any instrument. She had been calibrating it for a long time.

The door was unlocked. She went inside and closed the door behind her and stood in the kitchen for a moment, letting the room tell her what it had to say.

## VI.

Three bowls of porridge on the table, still steaming faintly. Three chairs — large, medium, small. Three of everything, arranged with the unconscious symmetry of a family that has lived together long enough for order to become instinct.

She tasted from the first bowl. Too hot, salted and rich, the man's portion. She set it back exactly as she had found it. Precision cost nothing and imprecision could cost everything.

She tasted from the second bowl. Too cold already, plain from the pot, the cook's portion. She set it back.

She sat in the small chair and ate from the third bowl — still warm, a little sweet, late-summer honey measured carefully. She ate without pleasure because pleasure was a distraction. It was fuel. When she finished she set the bowl back exactly where it had been and folded the cloth the same way Marta had folded it.

The drawing above the hearth. She looked at it and looked away.

Henrik's hunting knife on its peg near the door — too heavy, built for a hand larger than hers. She put it back. In a small wooden box on the windowsill, the boy's pocketknife — blade barely the length of her thumb, the handle carved with a fish that had started as a bear. She opened it and closed it. Too light.

Marta's cook's knife hung from its hook above the preparation board. Long and narrow, the blade kept bright and the edge kept true in the way of a knife sharpened regularly by someone who understands that a tool is only as good as its maintenance. She lifted it. The weight moved correctly in her hand — the balance right, the length right, the edge true. Not testing. Recognizing when she found just the right tool.

She took it upstairs and lay down on the smallest bed, on top of the blanket, the knife beside her right hand where she could find it without looking. She closed her eyes. The house settled around her, the banked fire breathing slow.

She was very good at waiting. The waiting was its own discipline — clearing the mind of everything except the present moment, not projecting forward, not reviewing backward, simply being in the room with the quality of a thing that belongs there. She waited.

## VII.

The Bär family came back in the middle of the afternoon, already talking as they came through the birch wood — about the berries, about the windfall Henrik had cleared, about a spider Pip had observed in the meadow grass with a web geometry he was describing in comprehensive detail. Henrik walked slightly ahead, thinking about Werner's letter. Marta walked between her husband and her son and listened to two things at once.

The sound of it — so domestic, so completely unguarded, the easy assumption in the voices that they were coming home to the home they had left — was the thing Elspeth upstairs always found hardest. Not the faces. The voices. The voices before they knew. She lay still and let the feeling come in only a little and then put it away.

Downstairs, the door opened. She heard Henrik's low sound of puzzlement. Marta going quiet in the specific way of someone who has moved from noticing to processing. Then Pip's voice, confused and not yet frightened: "Someone sat in my chair."

Then Marta said, quietly but with a clarity that carried: "Go outside, Pip. Stay in the garden. Do not go into the trees."

The door opened and closed. Two sets of footsteps on the stairs, deliberate and slow. The sleeping loft door opened. She opened her eyes.

Henrik filled the doorframe, the long saw still on his shoulder. Marta stood behind him and slightly to his left, her eyes already moving across the room with the systematic inventory of a woman assessing a situation. She was fast.

Elspeth had two seconds. She had planned for two seconds.

The cook's knife was under the blanket edge where her hand could find it without looking. She took him first because he was largest and because the saw in his hand was a problem if she gave him time to think about it. He went down hard against the doorframe and the sound of it was terrible and brief and then there was only Marta, who did not scream — she gave her that, she always gave them that when they didn't scream, it was the only thing she gave — but who had moved immediately for the window, the rational choice, and Elspeth had calculated for the rational choice.

The room when it was over was very quiet and very changed.

She washed her hands in the basin by the kitchen window, the water going dark, and dried them and folded the cloth back onto its hook. She checked the window glass. Pale hair, clear eyes. The dress still clean. She looked once more at the drawing above the hearth. She let the feeling in only a little. Then she went out into the afternoon.

Pip Bär was in the garden, crouched beside the herb beds, watching a beetle make its way across the worn wood of the step. The pocketknife open in his hand, still being used as a pointing device. He looked up when she came out.

She stopped. He was smaller than she had pictured from the boots — small-boned, dark-eyed, berry stains still on his chin from the high meadow. He looked at her with the open, undefended curiosity of a child who has not yet learned exactly what this moment required.

"Wer bist du?" he asked.

She looked at him for a moment. Somewhere in the Dunkelwald a wood thrush called once and fell silent.

She walked past him to the tree line without answering.

Behind her she heard him call — Mama? — in the ordinary tone of a child reporting something. Then again, louder, with the note of confusion. Then again, the word stretching and changing quality the way a word does when a child begins to understand that something is wrong without knowing what.

She walked into the Dunkelwald. The trees closed behind her.

In the garden, Pip Bär stood at the door of the cottage and called for his parents and received no answer, and called again, and the silence that came back was a new kind of silence, one he had never heard before, one he would spend the rest of his life recognizing in quiet rooms and empty hallways and the moment just before sleep when the world goes still and the mind, unbidden, goes back. He did not go inside. He stayed in the garden until dark, and then he curled under the kitchen window where the wall was still warm from the hearth, and he slept fitfully, and he woke, and he waited.

## VIII.

They found him on the third day. Oskar the charcoal-burner found him at dawn on the mill road, sitting with his boots on the wrong feet, his face perfectly still in a way that had nothing to do with calm. Oskar brought him inside and gave him warm milk and the boy sat at the table and stared at the cup and did not speak.

He did not speak that day. On the second afternoon, without looking up, he said: "sie hatte goldenes Haar." She had golden hair.

Oskar said nothing. He put another piece of wood on the fire and sat across the table from the boy and waited.

The woodsmen went in a group of seven. The cottage was exactly where the boy had described. The name carved into the lintel: Bär. The door unlocked. Inside, the porridge cold on the table. The drawing above the hearth, three round figures in charcoal on birch bark. The boots beside the door, Henrik's and Marta's, exactly where they had been left.

In the sleeping loft they found the small bed undisturbed — blanket smooth, pillow in its place — and on the pillow, set there with a deliberateness that excluded accident, was one of Pip's beetles. The iridescent one, the large one from the colony under the flat stone. Green-black, on its back, legs still. Placed with care, as if it mattered where exactly it was placed.

The seven men stood in the sleeping loft for a long time without speaking.

Afterward, Oskar said: "The most terrible thing was not what was in the loft. The most terrible thing was the basin by the window. The cloth beside it, used and then folded back onto its hook — neat, precise, as if what she had done was simply a task, and the task was finished, and the finishing of it required the same tidiness as everything else." No one argued with him.

Vogt came with his clipboard and performed an investigation that produced no result and that no one expected to produce a result, and that was the end of the official interest in what had happened to the Bär family.

Pip Bär grew up in the miller's household, quiet and careful, very good at reading rooms. He kept Werner's letter in his own coat pocket by the time he was fifteen. At nineteen he made his way to Hamburg and stood on the dock and waited for a ship with the combination of hope and resignation appropriate to an act you cannot undo once you commit to it. He arrived in New York harbor in the autumn of 1845, stood on the deck, and looked at a country that did not know his name yet. He changed Bär to Behr on arrival, because that was what the record-keeper wrote when he could not make the umlaut. Same sound in any mouth. Same bear at the center of it. Werner's letter had pointed him toward America. Mississippi was his own choice — the Delta was being rebuilt in the aftermath of the war, land was available to men willing to work hard country, and Pip Bär had never in his life been a man who chose the easier direction when the harder one pointed somewhere worth going. He went because he was his father's son and his father had been a man who moved toward the future however imperfectly it was available.

He never spoke of the Dunkelwald. But in his old age, when his grandchildren climbed into his lap and asked for a story, he told them about a family in a cottage in the wood — three bowls of porridge, three chairs, a boy child's bed, a girl with golden locks who had wandered in and run away frightened when the family came home. He let her go. In the story, he always let her go.

He never told them about Oskar, who checked the tree line on the mill road every afternoon for the rest of his life, who felt the hairs on his arms rise when the birches moved a certain way and a figure came through them into the light. He never told them that somewhere in the world, in all likelihood, there was still an unlocked door.

*— end of act one —*

# Act 2

## SHE CAME OUT OF THE COTTON

### I.

She came out of the cotton fields in the middle of the afternoon, when the light was still strong and the road back was easy to find. Her dress was clean. Pale gray, neat at the collar, not a mark on it. Her hair caught the light as she walked, very fair, loose around her shoulders and bright as field straw in the September sun — too bright, the kind of brightness that doesn't belong in a cotton field and announces itself whether you want to notice it or not.

An old man named Ezra, who lived in a one-room house near the Behr place — a house that had been old when the Behr children's grandfather was born — saw her come out of the far cotton fields near the road. He was sitting in his cane-bottomed chair in the shade of the chinaberry tree, the way he sat every afternoon. He would say later that he had felt her coming three days before she came — that the fields had a quality those three days that he had felt once before, in another county, forty years prior, and that the feeling had not been wrong then.

A girl coming out of the cotton. That hair — golden, he would say, golden locks loose around her face, the kind of hair that "don't belong in no cotton field" and you know it the minute you lay eyes on it. She did not look at him. She walked toward the Behr house with the brief, indifferent purpose of someone who does not intend to be remembered, and then she was up the porch steps and inside before he had fully decided what he was seeing.

Ezra sat in his chair and looked at the door she had gone through and then at the fields she had come out of. He was a man born at the tail end of Reconstruction in the Mississippi Delta and he had lived long enough to know what gathered dread felt like — the same tightening he had felt the last time he watched white men walking into the pines at dusk barely troubling to hide what they were carrying. He had not acted then either. He did not act fast enough now.

By then, of course, it was too late to think about anything useful.

* * *

Now go back. Go back to the beginning, which is to say go back to the morning, which is to say go back before the light shifted, before Ezra saw her, before anything was finished.

Go back to where it starts.

It always starts the same way.

## II.

Edmund Behr rose before the light.

It was a Tuesday in September, three days before she arrived, and Edmund had traplines to run along the Coldwater River before the sun came up and the day's real work began. He dressed in the dark the way he did everything — quietly, efficiently, with the economy of motion of a man who has learned not to waste anything. He went out across the yard and into the cotton fields heading east toward the river bottom, moving through the pre-dawn with the ease of a man who has walked the same ground so many times that his feet know it independent of his eyes.

The Coldwater ran through Quitman County with the slow authority of a river that has been where it is for a long time and intends to stay — brown and deep in the bends, quick and shallow over the gravel bars, cold in the mornings even in September, smelling of mud and vegetation and the specific mineral quality of Delta water that you either grew up with or you didn't. Edmund had grown up with it. He had run traplines on the Coldwater since he was twelve years old, and he knew the river's character in every season the way you know the character of something you have been in close relationship with for a long time.

The Delta in September morning has a quality of stillness that is not peace but resembles it closely enough to be mistaken for it, if you are not from here and do not know the difference. Edmund knew the difference. The land was flat in every direction and the sky came down to meet it without obstruction, and in the early morning before the heat began the light came in sideways across the cotton and made everything look briefly like it might be all right. It was not all right and had not been all right and he did not expect it to become all right. But it looked like it, in that light, for that hour. He had learned to take what was offered. He checked his lines with the efficiency of a man whose hands know the sequence without consulting him, moving downstream along the bank with the unhurried ease of a man who is exactly where he is supposed to be, doing exactly what he is supposed to be doing. It was the only hour of his day in which that was fully true. He had tried once to describe the smell of the river in the early morning to Mabel and had not found the words, and she had said: "I know." She had grown up on the same river half a county south. She did know. The knowing of it was one of the things they shared without needing to name.

He ran muskrats mostly, some fox, the occasional beaver in the slow bends. The pelts went to a buyer in Marks who paid less than they were worth because he could and because Edmund had no other buyer. The money went into the tin box under the loose board in the kitchen floor, added to the sharecrop money that remained after Pruitt took his share, building toward a number that Edmund checked every few weeks with the private arithmetic of a man calculating the distance between himself and something better. The land belonged to a man in Tunica — a Delta man, the kind who owned fields in three counties and visited none of them, who knew Pruitt's name and not Edmund's, whose relationship to the Coldwater River bottom was a line item in an account book kept in a comfortable office forty miles north. Edmund had never met him. He did not expect to.

He thought about Memphis on the walk back, the pelts over his shoulder, the sun coming up flat and red over the cotton. His cousin Dorsey had written from Memphis last spring. The letter said a man could be addressed as Mister on a Memphis street, that a man with a skill and a steady disposition could find work that paid wages instead of shares, that the schools were open and the children in them were learning. Gus was four. Edmund had done the arithmetic. He needed to be gone from Quitman County before Gus was old enough to understand what Quitman County's schools were saying to him about his own worth.

The buckboard was in the yard, the old mule Theodore hitched to the fence post and regarding the morning with his habitual philosophical resignation. Edmund unloaded the pelts and went to wash and came back and saw the footprints in the dust near the kitchen garden. He crouched and confirmed what he thought he knew. Two trips along the wall to the kitchen window. Luther Crane.

He was still at the pump when Crane came up the road.

He came the way he always came — no particular hurry, no particular direction, the walk of a man who has nowhere to be and has decided that this is as good a place as any to not be there. He had a way of arriving that made it difficult to say exactly when he had arrived, the way a bad smell has no precise moment of beginning. He stopped at the fence line and put one boot on the lowest rail and looked at the yard with the proprietary ease of a man assessing something he is considering acquiring.

Edmund straightened up from the pump and dried his hands on the cloth hanging from the nail and waited.

"Morning," Crane said.

"Morning," Edmund said. Neither of them looked away from the other and neither of them looked directly at the other, which was the grammar these exchanges required, in this county, in this year, between these two men.

Crane said: "You got any work needs doing — fence repair, ditch work, whatever you got."

"I appreciate you asking," Edmund said. "Nothing right now." He said it the way he said everything to Crane — evenly, without inflection, giving nothing that could be acted upon. The even tone cost him. It always cost him. There was a version of this conversation he could not have, a register he could not use, a directness unavailable to him by the specific legal and social architecture of the place and time he lived in.

Crane nodded. His eyes moved to the house, to the kitchen window, the way they always moved to the kitchen window when Mabel was inside — not a look but a returning, the eyes of a man going back to something he has already decided is his.

"I'll let you know if something comes up," Edmund said. The dismissal as neutral as everything else, as carefully constructed, as costly.

Crane took his boot off the fence rail. “You do that,” he said. He said it to Edmund but he was still looking at the kitchen window. Then he walked back up the road the way he had come, unhurried, in no particular direction, toward no particular place.

Crane had been coming around for two months. He was a white man from Alabama, moving through the county the way men move through a place when they have already been somewhere and been moved along. He had come through doing day work and had stayed longer than men like him usually stayed, moving his camp around in a pattern that had brought him closer and closer to the Behr place over two months. His face was disfigured along the left jaw — an old burn scar, smooth, pulling the corner of his mouth slightly in a way that made his expression hard to read. He was not large. He was not physically threatening in any conventional sense. What he was was a man with a fixed quality in his eyes, the look of someone who has decided the world owes him something specific and is patient about collecting it. He had fixed on Mabel.

Edmund stood up and went inside and said nothing to Mabel because saying something would have required her to respond and her response would have required him to act and his acting in Quitman County in 1931 on a matter of a white man’s attention toward his wife had exactly one possible legal outcome and it was not the outcome Edmund intended to bring on his family. He managed Crane the way Marta Bär had managed Vogt — with careful, neutral courtesy that gave nothing and refused nothing that could be acted upon. He watched him. He stayed between him and Mabel when he could. He hated doing it. He added it to the running total he kept against the day they would be gone.

Memphis, he thought, washing up at the pump. Gus’s school. A man treated like a man. Soon.

## III.

Mabel Behr ran her household with the organized precision of a woman who has understood from an early age that order is not a luxury but a form of resistance — that in a world arranged to tell you your house doesn’t matter and your things don’t matter and you don’t matter, keeping a clean house and a sharp knife and white curtains at the windows is a way of insisting otherwise. The shotgun house was three rooms deep and one room wide — front room, middle room, back room, straight through — and Mabel had arranged those three rooms as if the arrangements were an argument, because they were. The porch swept every morning. The Bible read from every morning before the work began. The curtains white and washed every Monday.

She kept her cook's knife — the long narrow one her mother had given her at her marriage, blade kept bright and edge kept true and sharpened every Sunday after reading and before breakfast — on the hook above the preparation board. A dull blade was more dangerous than a sharp one. Her mother had told her this and her mother's mother had told her mother, the kind of knowledge that travels in the hands and in the telling.

Gus was four years old, small-boned like Mabel and round-faced like Edmund and currently engaged in a detailed investigation of the beetle colony on the porch steps. His given name was Bruno — German for brown bear, though no one in the family knew this anymore, the meaning having been lost somewhere in the transit from one world to another, the name persisting after the meaning had gone the way names do. The world moved slow in the Delta heat and Bruno was a mouthful of Delta drawl, and so he was Gus.

Mabel watched him from the kitchen window — the careful crouch, the serious face, the way he observed a thing before touching it. He had his father's quality of attention. She hoped Edmund lived to see it fully developed. She thought about Memphis with the same practical attention she brought to everything. Not with hope. With arithmetic. The tin box under the floor. The number it needed to reach. She was a woman who managed things. She had always been a woman who managed things. She prayed in the morning and kept her house and sharpened her knife and managed things. She could not manage everything.

## IV.

Old Ezra had been on this land long enough that most people had stopped trying to calculate how long. He was old in ways that had passed through several distinct kinds of old and arrived somewhere beyond them — somewhere past white hair and slow movement, somewhere quieter and more permanent, the way certain trees look after enough years. He had outlasted categories.

He lived in his one-room house near the Behr place, and spent his days in the cane-bottomed chair that faced the cotton fields. He had a sense of the land's history that nobody else living shared, which gave his observations a weight that the people who knew him had learned to take seriously.

On the Monday of the week she came, he told Mabel: "Keep the boy on the porch this week. Keep him where you can see him."

"All right, Ezra," Mabel said. She said it the way you agree to things when you have decided to trust someone further than the available explanation warrants.

He told Gus separately, later: "You go home before dark, hear? Stay where your mama can see you this week."

"Yessir," Gus said. Then: "Why?"

"Cause I say so," Ezra said, "and that's enough why for right now." Gus accepted this with the complete trust of a child who has learned that this particular old man means what he says and has been right before.

He watched the fields all that week with the focused attention of a man who has felt a thing before and knows what feeling it again means. The quality was there — a heaviness at the field's edge, a particular stillness in the cotton rows. He had felt it before. Not this — not exactly this — but the shape of it, the gathering of something that had already decided what it was going to do and was simply moving toward the doing of it. He had been a young man the last time, standing at the edge of the road at dusk watching white men walk into the pine woods at the far end of the field, their robes not quite hidden, not even bothering to be quite hidden, because in Quitman County in those years the not-hiding was part of the message. He had stood at the edge of the road and felt the same tightening in his chest, the same knowledge arriving before he had words for it, the same question of whether he had the standing to act on what he knew. He had told himself he wasn't sure enough. He had not moved. He had carried what followed from that for forty years and he had never once in forty years believed his own excuse.

He was not going to carry another one. He was waiting for the certainty that would let him say something definitive to another man about his family. Certainty was taking its time arriving. He waited too long.

### V.

She had come to the edge of the cotton fields bordering the Behr place at dawn on the Monday and had spent three days reading the household before she moved. She watched Edmund cross to the river bottom before sunup. She watched Mabel on the porch, the curtains on the line, the kitchen garden worked in the early morning before the heat came. She watched Gus with his beetles on the porch steps. She watched the old man in the cane-bottomed chair under the chinaberry tree, and she noted him, and she assessed him.

He watched the fields. He watched them the way a man watches something he is expecting. She noted this as a complication, not a prevention. An old man with a feeling was not the same as an old man with a plan.

The gap was Tuesday afternoon: the family in Marks for the doctor, the house empty between two and four. She had confirmed this through three days of watching and through the conversation she had overheard between Edmund and Mabel on the porch Monday evening. She waited through Tuesday morning. She let the buckboard get far enough down the road that she could no longer hear the mule's footfall. Then she crossed the open ground toward the house.

She felt the old man's eyes on her back as she crossed the yard. She did not turn around. She went up the porch steps and tried the door. Unlocked. She understood why — a locked door in 1931 Quitman County on a Black family's shotgun house sent the wrong message to the wrong people. She did not let the understanding become comfortable. She went inside and closed the door behind her.

### VI.

Three covered pots on the stove, still warm from the morning's cooking. Three chairs at the table. Three of everything, arranged with the same unconscious symmetry she had seen long ago in the Bavarian cottage — the symmetry of a family that has lived together long enough for order to become instinct.

Edmund's portion on the back burner — pork and onions, heavily seasoned the way a man seasons food after a day in the field. Too much. She replaced the cloth exactly. The main pot, Mabel's portion — deep and complex, slow-cooked. Too rich. She replaced the lid. The small pot nearest the firebox — corn mush, soft and a little sweet, the child's portion. She sat in the small chair and ate it slowly. Fuel. When she finished she replaced the cloth and folded it the same way Mabel had folded it.

The child's drawing on the wall beside the window — three figures in pencil on the back of a flour sack, round and earnest, slightly too large for their legs, standing in front of a house. The same three figures, the same house. Different hand. Different surface. The same essential thing. She looked at it for a moment and looked away.

Edmund's hunting knife near the door — too heavy. In a tobacco tin on the shelf, the boy's pocketknife with its handle wrapped in twine where it had cracked — too small. She opened it and closed it and set it back. Mabel's cook's knife hung from the hook above the preparation board. She lifted it. The weight moved correctly in her hand — the same recognition, every time, the same settling of the balance, the same sense of a tool that has been kept as a tool should be kept. Just right for what she intended. She took it to the back room and lay down on the child's quilt and closed her eyes and waited.

In the cotton fields outside, the September afternoon moved slowly. A mockingbird ran through its catalog somewhere in the chinaberry tree. The old man in his cane-bottomed chair looked at the door of the house and could not make himself move fast enough.

## VII.

The Behr family came back from Marks in the middle of the afternoon, the buckboard raising a thin trail of dust on the road from town. Gus pronounced healthy, feet needing new shoes. Edmund had sold the pelts and bought the shoes — brown leather, solid at the toe, a size bigger than needed because feet grow. Mabel had bought cloth and, after a moment of hesitation Edmund saw and noted, a small paper bag of boiled sweets that Gus had been eyeing without saying so.

Gus had a boiled sweet on his tongue and new shoes already dusty when they came up from the road, running ahead the way he always ran. They were talking as they came — about the doctor, about the cloth pattern, about Theodore's left foreleg — and the sound of it, three voices in domestic transit, so unguarded, was the thing Elspeth in the back room always found hardest. Not the faces. The voices. She lay still on the child's quilt and let the feeling in only a little and then put it away.

Then the door opened. The sounds of entry moved through the house toward her — footsteps on the wooden floor, front room, middle room, stopping. Edmund's low sound of puzzlement. Mabel going still in the specific way. Then Gus's voice, confused and not yet frightened: "Somebody ate my mush."

Mabel said, with a quietness that carried its own weight: "Go outside, Gus. Stay on the porch. Don't go near the river."

She heard the small argument forming in Gus's voice and then swallowed, and then the door, and then two sets of adult footsteps moving through the shotgun house — front room, middle room, back room, the floor plan offering no detours. The back room door opened. She opened her eyes.

Edmund filled the doorframe, broad through the chest and shoulders. Behind him Mabel stood with her hand on the doorframe, her eyes already moving, already calculating. She was fast. It was not fast enough.

The cook's knife was under the quilt edge where her hand could find it. She took him first because he was largest. He went down hard against the doorframe and the sound of it was terrible and brief and then there was only Mabel, who did not scream — she gave her that, she always gave them that when they didn't scream — who moved immediately for the window, the rational choice, and Elspeth had calculated for the rational choice.

The room when it was over was very quiet and very changed.

She washed her hands and dried them and folded the cloth back onto its hook. She checked the window glass. Pale hair, clear eyes. The dress still clean. She looked once more at the drawing on the flour sack. Then she went through the house and out onto the porch.

Gus Behr was on the porch steps, crouched over a boll weevil making its way across the worn wood of the second step — the small curved unmistakable shape of it, the insect that had been breaking the Delta for fifteen years, worked through the cotton rows with patient indifference to what its presence cost the people who had planted them. He looked up when she came out.

She stopped. Small-boned, round-faced, a boiled sweet on his chin. He looked at her with the open, undefended curiosity of a child who has not yet learned the category.

"Who are you?" he asked.

She looked at him for a moment. A redbird called once from the chinaberry tree and fell silent.

She walked past him into the yard and toward the far cotton fields without answering. Behind her she heard him call — Mama? — in the ordinary tone of a child reporting something. Then again, louder. Then again, the word changing shape the way a word does when a child starts to understand that something is wrong. She walked into the cotton. The rows closed around her. She walked until the house was out of sight, until there was only cotton in every direction, and then she kept walking.

In the yard behind her, Gus Behr stood on the porch steps and called for his parents and received no answer, and called again, and the silence that came back was a new kind of silence. One he had never heard before. One he would spend the rest of his life recognizing.

## VIII.

Ezra found Gus at first light, sitting on the porch step with his new shoes on the wrong feet, staring at the door. He brought him inside and wrapped him in a quilt and gave him water and the boy sat at the small table and stared at the cup and did not speak. He did not speak that first day. On the second afternoon, without looking up, he said: "She had golden hair."

"I know it," Ezra said. He said it quietly, in the voice of a man confirming something he already knew, which was its own kind of terrible thing to say.

They went in a group — because what a group of Black men could do in Quitman County in 1931 about anything involving a white girl was a number that had to be calculated carefully, and the number was very small, and they went anyway because Ezra asked them to and because the Behr family deserved to have someone bear witness even if bearing witness was all that could be done.

In the back room of the shotgun house, on the pillow of the child's bed, set there with the same deliberate care as everything else she did, was a boll weevil. The small curved shape of it, placed on its back, legs still. The insect that had been bankrupting their county, placed on the pillow of the child of a family that had been surviving that bankruptcy one careful season at a time.

That evening Ezra sat alone at his small table with the lamp burning between his hands. He had been to the shotgun house with the others. He had seen what there was to see. He had brought Gus back with him and settled the boy on the pallet and watched him fall into the fitful sleep of a child whose body has given out before his mind has caught up with what his mind is going to have to carry.

He sat at the table and thought about what he would have said to Edmund if Edmund had been able to come to him. He had been carrying something for forty years that he had never told anyone, and now the man he would have told it to was gone, and the telling was going to stay inside him where it had always been, one more thing he had not done in time.

He thought about the men walking into the pines. He thought about what he had failed to do then and what he had failed to do this week. He sat with both failures in the lamplight and did not try to weigh one against the other because that was not a weighing he had any right to do. The lamp burned down. He sat in the dark. Then he went to bed.

In the morning he went to check on Gus.

Ezra lived to see another year. He died in his cane-bottomed chair in the April of the following spring, facing the cotton fields, in the attitude of a man who has set down a watch he has kept for a very long time. At his graveside, an old woman said to another old woman: "He knew she was coming. Said he seen her before." The second woman nodded and asked no further questions.

## IX.

Luther Crane was gone from the county before the end of the month. Nobody went looking for him. Nobody went looking for her. The investigation produced the result such investigations produced in Quitman County in 1931 when the family in question was the family in question.

Gus spent the first months after in Ezra's house, the old man tending him with the patient attention of someone who knows he has limited time and intends to use it correctly. When Ezra died the following

April, his daughter took the boy in and raised him there, in the same house, in the same chair's shadow, so that Gus grew up in Ezra's house after all — just not with Ezra in it. He grew up knowing what kind of silence he was in before anyone told him. He left Quitman County in his young manhood and followed the Illinois Central north to Memphis, which felt like a destination he had been moving toward his whole life, because he had been. He changed the spelling, Behr to Baer, one more small adjustment on the long journey from a Bavarian forest to a Memphis neighborhood. Same sound. Same bear. He built a life in Binghamton and was the best version of himself that the available circumstances permitted.

He never spoke of the shotgun house on the Coldwater River. But in his old age, when his grandchildren climbed into his lap and asked him for a story, he told them about a family at the edge of the cotton fields, and a girl who came in through the unlocked door. Three covered pots. Three chairs. A boy child's bed. The girl ran away frightened when the family came home safe. He let her go. In the story, he always let her go.

He never told them about old Ezra, watching the cotton fields from his cane-bottomed chair every afternoon until the spring of the year he died. He never told them that somewhere in the world, in all likelihood, there was still an unlocked door.

*— end of act two —*

# Act 3

## TILLMAN STREET

### I.

She came into the parking lot of the Tillman Arms in the middle of a January afternoon, when the light was already going thin and the temperature had dropped eight degrees since noon. Her coat was wrong for the weather — too light, a summer weight, pale and clean. Her hair caught what was left of the afternoon light as she crossed the lot, very fair, loose around her shoulders and bright as something that had no business being that bright in a Memphis January. She was looking at her phone with the focused attention of someone who already knows exactly where she is.

Two old men were sitting in the covered walkway outside apartment 2B — Mr. Calvin Priest and Mr. Darnell Webb, who had been playing checkers in that walkway every afternoon the weather permitted since approximately 1983, when Calvin had moved into the Tillman Arms and found Darnell already there with the board set up, and had sat down, and had not found any sufficient reason to stop in the years since. Between them they had watched the Tillman Arms and the Binghamton neighborhood change in the gradual, bureaucratic way that neighborhoods get written off — the slow withdrawal of services, the streetlights that took longer to fix, the bus routes that got adjusted in ways that added time to every trip.

Calvin was studying the board with the focused attention of a man who takes the game seriously even after thirty years. Darnell saw her.

He watched her cross to the building entrance. An older woman was coming out. The girl held the door with a brief smile and slipped inside before the door had finished closing. "Your move," Calvin said.

Darnell looked at the door where she had been. He picked up a checker piece and held it without moving it.

"Darnell."

"That girl."

Calvin looked at the closed door. "What girl?"

"The one just went in. Yellow hair. Pale coat."

"I was looking at the board," Calvin said.

Darnell set the piece down in the wrong square. He never set pieces down in the wrong square. He said, slowly: "My grandmother used to tell a story. About a family. And a girl with hair like that. She grew up in Marks. In Marks there were stories about a family named Behr and a girl who came out of the cotton one September afternoon a long time ago."

Calvin waited. Darnell didn't continue. "And?" Calvin said.

"It wasn't a good story," Darnell said.

He stood up. "Marcus Baer still leaving that boy home alone this week?"

"School's closed all week," Calvin said. "Both of them working. You know how it is."

"Mm hmm," Darnell said. He stood at the edge of the covered walkway and looked at the door of the building for a long time. Then he went inside.

He stood in his kitchen with his hand on the phone and thought about what he would say, and could not find the words, and put the phone down. He made himself coffee. He sat at his kitchen table and listened to the sounds of the building and told himself he was not sure enough. He told himself he needed to be sure before he said something that would sound crazy. He was not going to be free of that either.

* * *

Now go back. Go back to the beginning, which is to say go back to the morning, which is to say go back before she arrived, before any of this was finished.

Go back to where it starts.

It always starts the same way.

## II.

Deja Baer woke at four forty-five on the days she worked the early shift, which was most days, because the EVS supervisor at Methodist

Central had a gift for scheduling that favored the people he liked and burdened the people he didn't, and Deja had made the mistake early in her tenure of doing her work too well, which meant she was reliable, which meant she got the assignments the less reliable people couldn't be trusted with.

EVS stood for Environmental Services, which was the hospital's name for the work of keeping the building clean — the patient rooms, the hallways, the surgery suites where things happened that had to be made to not have happened before the next shift came on. Essential work done by people who were treated as though it were barely work at all by most of the people above them in the hierarchy. Deja had made her peace with this in the particular way you make peace with things you cannot change and choose not to be destroyed by.

The supervisor's name was Mr. Dewaine Pickett, but on the floor he was known as Janitor Number One, which was not his actual job classification on the Methodist Central organizational chart. It was how the EVS crews rendered it in the break room shorthand with an emphasis that made clear that everyone understood the irony. He was a tall odd-shaped man in his late forties with a clipboard he didn't need and the aggrieved quality of someone who has done the arithmetic on what the world owes him and found the balance perpetually insufficient. He exercised his authority over eight women and two men with the thoroughness of someone for whom authority is the primary available satisfaction.

The women on his crew had developed a monitoring system for his moods as precise as a weather service. The intelligence was exchanged in the break room before shift, delivered in the flat tones of people reporting weather. "He took it last night" meant he had taken his ED medication and things had gone well, which meant a manageable day. "He didn't" was the other report meaning things had not gone well, meaning the frustration was still looking for somewhere to go, meaning keep your head down and give him nothing to find. They didn't really know what happened in the Pickett house, of course, but it was one of those things you sense when you work with frustrated, moody middle-aged men long enough.

Deja had learned to make herself unremarkable in his presence. To move through his field of attention without snagging on anything. He found things anyway, because finding things was not about the work. He would inspect a room she had cleaned perfectly and identify the corner she had missed, the surface she hadn't addressed, the documentation entry that wasn't wrong but that could be written better if he had written it. She absorbed the findings without visible reaction because reacting was the response he was looking for, and she had decided not to give it to him. It cost her something, the absorbing. She was not a woman built for smallness. She compressed those qualities for eight hours and then she got on the MATA 43 Line bus down Poplar with her Methodist Central lanyard still around her neck and she came home.

Coming home was the reason for the compression. Coming home was what the compression made possible.

On the Tuesday in January that Elspeth came, Janitor Number One had been in a middling state — not the ease of a good morning, not the full weight of a bad one, just the low simmering irritability of a man in the middle of his own unrequited private situation. He had inspected her wing twice and found nothing useful and had finally written her up for a documentation entry she had filled in correctly but in blue ink on a form that specified black. She had signed the write-up without comment and without expression and had gone back to her wing.

She had been thinking about Marcus's beans on the stove. About Orson's math worksheet that she had promised to look over. About taking her shoes off at her own front door.

At two-thirty the Facilities Director appeared at the end of her wing — unusual enough that she looked up. "You've got your hours banked, Deja," he said. "Take the rest of the day." She looked at him for a moment. She took off her gloves. She texted Marcus — coming home early, xoxo — and was already moving before she pressed send. She did not stop long at the locker room. She walked past Janitor Number One's office in the hall and did not look in. He was at his desk with his clipboard and did not look up. He never knew what he was part of. Neither did the Facilities Director.

The 43 ran down Poplar from the medical district through Midtown and into Binghamton, the same route every day, the same stops, the same quality of afternoon light through scratched windows that Deja had been reading for three years like a text she knew by heart. She knew which stop smelled like the dry cleaner's exhaust and which one smelled like the Tops Bar-B-Q two blocks over, the specific geography of the city delivered to her nose before her eyes confirmed it. She knew the regulars — the older man with the newspaper who got on at Cleveland and folded it to the crossword without looking up, the woman with the grocery bags who took the seat behind the driver and talked to him about her grandchildren whether he responded or not, the teenagers from the high school who filled the back with noise and then drained out at the East Parkway stop leaving a quiet that felt like a different kind of noise.

January light in Memphis has a quality particular to itself — thin and pale and coming in at an angle that makes everything look slightly more honest than it wants to be, the old houses in Midtown with their wide porches and their peeling paint catching that light and giving it back without flattery. She loved those houses. She had grown up wanting to live in one of those houses, the ones with the craftsman details and the deep lots and the magnolias that went sixty feet in the air and dropped their leaves all winter like they didn't care what anyone thought. She and Marcus had talked about it — someday, after the degree, after the promotion, after Orson was through school and the numbers worked differently than they worked now. Someday was a real place in their shared geography. They visited it regularly.

She still had her Methodist Central lanyard around her neck. She tucked it inside her coat the way she always did when she got on the bus, not out of embarrassment but out of the specific privacy of a woman who has been institutional property for eight hours and is now, for the duration of this ride, nobody's anything. Just a woman on the 43 going home. The compression socks were still on her feet. She would take them off at her own front door, the first act of being home, the small ceremony of it.

The city moved past the window. The AutoZone on Poplar. The church with the marquee that changed its message every week to something that was either profound or mildly threatening depending on your mood when you read it. The used car lot with the flags that snapped in the January wind. The Mapco where Marcus sometimes stopped for gas on the way home from the medical center, where the man behind the counter knew him by name and asked about Orson's football, and where Marcus always bought a scratch-off ticket that never won anything and that he scratched in the parking lot before he drove away, because that was how you did it — you scratched it while you still believed.

She got off at Poplar and Tillman and crossed Poplar — six lanes plus a turn lane, one of the busiest streets in Memphis, the kind of thoroughfare that doesn't slow down for January or for pedestrians or for anything that isn't another car — and walked the three blocks north to the Tillman Arms with her hands in her pockets and her chin down against the raw January cold, the kind that settles into the Mid-South and finds every gap in your coat and stays there. To her right as she crossed, set back on its generous lot on Poplar Avenue, was the Benjamin Hooks Central Library — a building she had walked past a hundred times, that she registered the way you register a building that has always been there, as a feature of the landscape rather than a place that holds anything particular. She did not know that on the fourth floor of that building, in the genealogy section that smells of old paper and microfilm and the particular stillness of a room where people come to find things they are not always prepared to find, her husband's family's name existed in a record she had never seen and would never see, waiting for someone to find it. She did not know and had no reason to know and walked past it the way she walked past it every day, already thinking about beans and math worksheets and compression socks, already home in her mind before her feet had gotten her there.

The parking lot of the Tillman Arms was half empty in the pale January afternoon. Calvin and Darnell in the covered walkway, the checkerboard between them. She raised a hand. Calvin raised one back. She pushed through the front door into the warmth of the building and thought about Marcus's beans and Orson's math worksheet and taking her shoes off, in that order, the liturgy of coming home.

### III.

Marcus Baer was thirty-four years old and broad through the chest and shoulders and had spent eleven years loading and unloading supply trucks at the Regional Medical Center with the steady, uncomplaining competence of a man who has made a clear-eyed distinction between the work he currently has and the work he intends to have, and who is moving from the first toward the second with deliberate patience.

He drove to work in the 1982 Cadillac Fleetwood that had been his father Gus's and was now his — long and dark and maintained with the particular devotion of a man who has been given something by someone he loved and intends for the giving to mean something. Not practical. Too much gas, parts getting hard to source, the last alternator job involving a three-week search that ended with a parts dealer in Kentucky who still had original stock. He drove it anyway, because his father had driven it and because some inheritances are worth their cost.

On Tuesday and Thursday evenings Marcus was at the University of Memphis for his civil engineering coursework, five-thirty to nine-thirty, a class with a lab that ran the full four hours. He had enrolled three years ago, working toward a degree that was going to take six years at the pace he could afford — a full shift at The Med, home by four to start dinner and get Orson fed, Deja in by mid-afternoon on her early shift days so the three of them had a brief window together at the table before Marcus was back out the door and a three-mile drive that might as well have been another country to a classroom where he was usually the oldest person present and was always the most prepared. He came home at ten to a quiet house, Deja and Orson already asleep, and stood in the kitchen for a few minutes eating whatever was left and listening to the building settle before he went to bed.

On Sunday mornings Marcus cooked. Red beans and rice he had started the night before with the kidney beans soaking, the trinity done slow and deliberate until they were soft and sweet, the andouille added early so the fat rendered into the base, the whole pot going by seven so it had all day. It was not a fast meal. That was the point. Some things were worth the time they took.

He had portioned the beans on Monday evening: his own portion covered and set on the back burner, seasoned the way he liked it — more cayenne, more thyme. Deja's in the main pot. Orson's in the small, covered bowl, mild and just right, because Orson had declared at age six that he did not like things on his food and Marcus had chosen to respect this declaration, on the grounds that Orson was right that food was his food and he should have a say in it.

He had kissed Deja at five-fifteen in the morning, still mostly asleep, feeling her move away from him toward the door with the specific purposeful efficiency of a woman who has seventeen things to do before she gets on the bus, and had gone back to sleep for the forty minutes remaining before his own alarm. He was at The Med by seven. He would be home by three-thirty. He did not know yet that three-thirty was going to be six minutes too late, and that six minutes was going to be the measure of a life.

**IV.**

Darnell Webb's grandmother had been born in Marks, Mississippi, in the last decade of the nineteenth century, to a woman who had been born enslaved and who carried in her memory a history that she dispensed in careful portions to the people she loved, giving them what they needed and not more. She had grown up in the same community that absorbed Gus Behr after the September of 1931 — the same tight world of Quitman County where stories traveled in the careful partial way that people pass on things they cannot fully explain and cannot afford to forget. She had not known the Behr family directly. She had known the story of them, the way you know the stories that a community carries without quite being able to say where they started or who first told them. A family on the Coldwater. A girl with golden hair who came out of the cotton. Two people dead and a child left on the porch. The story had traveled the way it needed to travel — not loudly, not completely, but in the way of a warning passed hand to hand until the original source is lost and only the warning remains.

Darnell's grandmother had told him the story when he was twelve years old, on the porch of her house in Marks on a summer evening when the fireflies were starting up in the yard. She was a very old woman by then, with the directness of a woman who had lived long enough to know what required words and what didn't. She told it once, directly, trusting him to receive it.

She said: "There is a family. Got a name that sounds like bear. German-style name. They been followed a long time, longer than I know, and I know some things about long times. If you ever come across that name — hear me, Darnell, I mean hear me — you pay attention to it. You don't wait. Whatever you feel, you act on it. You don't wait for more."

He had been twelve. He had filed it in the category of things his grandmother told him that he didn't understand yet. She had a number of items in that category. They had all turned out to mean something eventually.

He had filed the name Baer away when Marcus and Deja moved into 1C six years ago. He had noted it and had watched the family across six years with the patient attention of a man keeping a watch he had been assigned. The Cadillac in the parking lot, maintained beyond all practicality. The smell of red beans on Sunday morning that came through the walls. Orson's laugh, loud and total, the laugh of a child who had not yet learned to modulate it.

The girl with the golden hair crossing the parking lot on a January afternoon was what registering it meant.

He knew it in the moment he saw her, with the specific clarity of a thing coming into focus — not alarm, not fear, but recognition. His grandmother's voice: "You don't wait. Whatever you feel, you act on it."

He had stood in his kitchen with his hand on the phone for twenty minutes. He had not acted. He had waited for words that would not come, for certainty that would not come, for something more than a feeling and his grandmother's voice. His grandmother had told him not to wait for more. She had known that more would not arrive in time. He was going to have to live with that, the way Ezra had lived with it, the way Oskar had lived with it, the way every man on the margin in every iteration of this story had lived with the weight of having known and not moved fast enough.

**V.**

She had been watching the Tillman Arms for four days before she moved, circulating through the Binghamton neighborhood with the unhurried quality of someone in transit. Memphis was good for this. A young woman with fair hair on an errand that was nobody's business was simply part of the city's texture.

She had confirmed the family's schedule on three separate days. The father in the Cadillac by seven. The mother on the 43 line at four forty-five, hospital worker, early shift. The boy alone in the apartment all week, school closed. She had noted the two old men in the covered walkway and assessed them across four days. The one who talked had not looked up from the board. The one who did not talk had looked at her on the first and second and fourth days. More looking than most people did. She assessed him as perceptive but not actionable. An old man with a feeling. She had been wrong about this assessment exactly once, in another city, in another decade, when an old man with a feeling had moved fast enough to prevent what she had come to do. She had not been able to do what she had come to do and had left with nothing, and she thought about that failure the way she thought about all her failures — directly, as information about what to calculate for next time. She did not know she was wrong again.

The outer door required social engineering. An older woman coming out, a held door, a brief smile. Inside. The apartment door was locked, as she had known. She knocked. A pause. Then the boy's voice, careful, not coming to the door: "Manager's in 1A." "Thank you," she said. "I'm so sorry to bother you." She listened to his footsteps retreat. Then she moved along the exterior wall to the kitchen window she had identified on the second day, the one with the aging latch that had a specific play in it. She worked it correctly. She had time. She went in through the kitchen window and closed it behind her with the same care she used closing every door, every window, every lid she replaced, every cloth she folded and set back. She stood in the kitchen of apartment 1C and looked at the room.

The bean pot on the back burner. The main pot covered. The small bowl covered on the counter. On the refrigerator, a magnet from Memphis, a drawing in crayon on construction paper — three figures round and earnest, slightly too large for their legs. OUR FAMLY in a child's block letters. She looked at it for a moment. Then she went into the living room.

## VI.

Orson Baer was nine years old and was currently applying his mother's organized precision and his father's deliberate quality to a sixth-grade math worksheet about fractions with unlike denominators that was giving him more trouble than he thought it should. He heard the voice at the door and answered it without getting up because the rule was clear: you can answer questions through the door, you do not open the door for anyone who is not on the approved list. He gave the information through the door and went back to the worksheet.

He heard the sound from the direction of the kitchen four minutes later. Small, mechanical, the sound of the kitchen window latch worked from outside. His body named it before his mind did. He looked up.

She was in the kitchen doorway. Pale dress. Golden hair loose around her shoulders, bright in the dim January apartment in a way that was wrong for the available light. Smaller than he had somehow expected. A face that was ordinary in every feature and that he could not find anything in to hold onto, no landmark, no expression, no reflection of the room.

She moved to the kitchen counter. Not toward him. She lifted the cloth on the back burner. Looked at it and replaced the cloth exactly as it had been. Lifted the lid on the main pot and replaced it. Stood before his bowl and lifted the cloth and looked at it for a long moment. Then she came into the living room and sat down on his end of the couch — the middle cushion, the one with the slight collapse from use, where he always sat.

She looked at his Chromebook and said, in a voice that was quiet and unremarkable: "What are you working on?"

"Math," he said.

"What kind?"

"Fractions."

"Do you like math?" He considered this. "I like how it's always the same," he said, before he had decided whether to say it. "Like if you know the rules it works the same every time no matter what."

Something moved in her face then — briefly, controlled, the way a feeling moves across a face when the person has become very practiced at not letting feelings move across their face but has not quite managed to prevent this particular one. It was there and then it was gone. "Yes," she said. "I understand that."

She sat with him for twenty minutes. She did not touch him. She asked him questions about school and about what he was going to do when he grew up, the ordinary questions adults ask children, delivered in the same quiet voice. He answered them the way a child answers questions when something in the room is wrong in a way he cannot name and he is using the sound of his own voice to take the measure of how wrong. He was watching the door. He had decided that when his father's key turned in the lock he was going to run.

He glanced once at the drawing on the refrigerator — OUR FAMLY, the MEMPHIS magnet, the three round figures. He did not let himself look at it for long.

"Who are you, ma'am?" he asked.

She looked at him. She did not answer. She stood up from the couch and moved toward the kitchen and he pulled his feet up under him and watched her go.

## VII.

Marcus Baer turned his key in the lock of apartment 1C at three twenty-nine in the afternoon and pushed the door open and said, automatically, the way he said it every day: "Orson, I'm home —"

He stopped.

The girl on the couch turned and looked at him. Pale dress. Golden hair. A face that registered as ordinary until you tried to find something in it and found nothing — no landmark, no way in, no reflection of what was happening in the room.

Orson was already in motion. He had heard the key in the lock and he had heard the half-beat in his father's voice — the break in the sentence that meant his father had seen something and had stopped — and his body had processed both pieces of information before his conscious mind caught up. He was off the couch and behind his father before Marcus had completed his first step into the apartment.

Marcus put his hand on his son's shoulder without looking at him. He did not take his eyes off the girl. "Who are you?"

"I was looking for the manager's office," she said. "Your son told me which apartment. I was just warming up while I waited."

"Orson."

"I didn't open the door, Daddy," Orson said. "She came through the kitchen window."

Marcus looked at the kitchen. He looked at his portion on the back burner and at the position of the cloth, which was not quite the position Deja had left it in. He knew how Deja left things. He had lived with how Deja left things for long enough to know. Every time. It never changed.

"Orson. Go to Mr. Darnell's apartment. Knock loud. Don't stop knocking until he opens the door."

"Daddy —"

"Right now, son. Go now."

He felt his son leave from behind him. He heard Orson's footsteps in the hall, moving fast. He heard the knock on 2B, both fists. He did not look away from the girl.

She stood up from the couch. She moved toward the kitchen with the unhurried ease of someone who has made all the relevant calculations and is now simply executing them. He moved to stay between her and the front door and she looked at him with that face and said, in a voice that was quiet and not unkind, the kindness making it worse somehow: "You should go too."

"This is my house," he said.

"I know," she said.

She glanced at the refrigerator. The MEMPHIS magnet. OUR FAMLY. The three round figures in Orson's careful crayon. She looked at it for a moment and then looked away and opened the kitchen drawer.

The chef's knife was in the drawer where it always was — the one good knife in the kitchen, long and narrow, the blade Deja kept bright and the edge she sharpened every Sunday, the knife she had bought herself when they first moved into this apartment because she believed in having one good knife and maintaining it properly. Elspeth lifted it from the drawer. She did not try the other knives first. She did not set it down and pick up another. There was no audition, no sequence, no too-heavy and too-light and just right. She simply opened the drawer and took the knife that was there and it moved correctly in her hand and she did not require more information than that.

The directness of it was its own kind of terrible. The efficiency was worse than a ritual would have been.

Marcus Baer looked at her. The knife. The face with nothing in it. He was thirty-four years old and had spent eleven years loading weight and was broad through the chest and had his son's footsteps still going fast in the hallway outside. He looked at what was in front of him and he made the calculation that he made, which was the calculation of a man who has sent his son to safety and is now in the room alone with this, and he stood his ground.

The weight of the knife moved correctly in her hand. The way it always did. The way it always had.

## VIII.

What happened in apartment 1C of the Tillman Arms on the afternoon of that January Tuesday is described in a Memphis Police Department incident report in the flat factual language that official reports use when the facts are sufficient and the facts are terrible. I obtained the report through a public records request filed from an office two blocks away on Tillman Street, where I had kept a desk for twenty years. I have read it many times. I have not been able to stop.

The report describes what was found in apartment 1C in the flat language reports use when the facts are sufficient. Marcus Baer, age thirty-four, was found in the kitchen. Deja Baer, age thirty-one, was found near the front door. Both had been stabbed. The weapon was a kitchen knife recovered at the scene. It was a good knife, well-maintained, the kind that settles into the hand like it was made for it. The report noted that it had been kept in the drawer beside the stove.

What the report does not contain is what happened before the police arrived, when Deja Baer came through the front door of the Tillman Arms with her Methodist Central lanyard still around her neck.

She came through the front door and down the ground-floor hallway and stopped in front of the door of apartment 1C, which was standing open in the specific way a door stands open when the person who passed through it last did not have a hand free to pull it shut. She stood in the hallway and looked at the open door. The hallway was quiet. The building had a quality of quiet she had not heard before — not the ordinary afternoon quiet of a residential building, but something underneath that, something in the air.

She was a woman who had spent three years reading the sounds of that building the way she read Janitor Number One's moods — with the systematic attention of someone whose safety depends on early information. She knew what the building sounded like at three in the afternoon. She knew what her apartment sounded like from the hallway when everything was as she had left it. This was not that.

She thought about Orson. She thought about Marcus. She went inside.

The knowing arrived correctly. It arrived at the point of her own favorite kitchen knife in the hands of a golden-haired young woman in a pale dress.

Darnell Webb heard the first silence through the wall of apartment 2B at three seventeen. He was in the hallway before he had consciously decided to move. Orson Baer was already there, both fists on the door of 2B, knocking the way Marcus had told him to knock — loud and without stopping. Darnell opened the door and the boy fell forward and Darnell caught him under both arms and brought him inside.

He locked the deadbolt and the chain. He brought Orson to the kitchen table and sat him down. The checkerboard was still there from this afternoon, including the piece Darnell had set down in the wrong square. He picked up his phone and called 911 and said, in a voice he made steady by deciding to make it steady: "I need you to send someone to apartment 1C at the Tillman Arms on Tillman Street. Something has happened. Please send someone now."

He set the phone down. He looked at Orson. The boy was looking at the checkerboard with his face absolutely still, in a way that had nothing to do with calm, in the way Darnell had heard about a child's face go still in Marks, a boy sitting in a road with his shoes on backwards. "Your daddy was a good man," Darnell said. He said it because it was true and because it was the only thing he had to give.

Orson did not look up.

Then Darnell heard the second silence through the wall. Different from the first in quality but identical in what it meant. He looked at the door of his own apartment, at the deadbolt and the chain, and then at the boy at the table. He reached across the checkerboard and moved the piece back to where it was supposed to be. He left his hand on the board for a moment. Then he stood up and put his back against the door and waited for the sirens, which came six minutes later, which was too late for what had already happened and exactly in time for what had not.

His grandmother's voice was in the room with him. It had been in the room with him since the moment he saw her cross the parking lot. He did not think it was going to leave.

## IX.

The security camera at the Tillman Arms entrance recorded her leaving the building at three twenty-two in the afternoon. The investigating officer noted that he watched the footage four times before writing his report. Pale dress. Golden hair. Nothing on the dress. She walked across the parking lot with the unhurried ease of someone who has completed what they came to do. At the corner where the lot met Tillman Street she paused and appeared to look at her phone and then walked out of the camera's frame. They canvassed the neighborhood for two days. No one had seen where she went. The descriptions were consistent and useless. Nothing in her face you could hold onto. They never found her.

* * *

The investigating officer filed a supplementary report the following morning noting one additional detail he had found difficult to categorize. On the pillow of the child's bed in apartment 1C — the bed belonging to Orson Baer, age nine — there was a single bed bug. Not a dead one, not a molt, not the evidence of an infestation. One live specimen, placed on its back on the center of the pillow, legs still.

The investigating officer noted that the apartment was immaculate. He had inspected apartments for twenty years and this one was in the top tier of what he had seen. There was no infestation in the building. The building manager confirmed this. The supplementary report noted the detail and made no interpretation of it. There was no interpretation available within the categories the report was designed to use.

Deja Baer had kept the cleanest apartment in the Tillman Arms. Everyone who had been inside it knew this. She had built something in those three rooms — the same thing Mabel Behr had built with white curtains and a swept porch, the same thing Marta Bär had built with graduated boots by the door and porridge seasoned three ways. The same conviction, in three different times and three different places, that order was a form of insistence on one's own worth.

One bed bug. On its back. Legs still.

* * *

The boy grew up with his mother's people in North Memphis, in the company of a family that forms around a loss when the loss is too strange to be explained directly and has to be absorbed instead. He grew up quiet and careful and very good at reading rooms. He grew up with a specific attentiveness to the sounds a building makes when everything is normal, because he had learned at nine years old that you could tell the difference between normal quiet and the other kind if you had been paying attention long enough to know what normal sounded like.

He left Memphis in his early twenties and went to New York. He became a civil engineer — the structures that bear load over time, the calculations of stress and force and the correct response to forces that act on a thing continuously and without mercy. He was good at it. He had his father's deliberate quality and his mother's organized precision and the quality of someone who has learned, not from a textbook but from experience, what it costs when a structure fails.

He has children now. They are young enough to want bedtime stories. He tells them about a family who lived in an apartment in the city — three covered pots on the stove, too spicy and too rich and just right, three chairs, a girl who came in through the window and ran away frightened when the family came home safe. He gives her a name borrowed from her hair. He lets her go. In the story, he always lets her go. His children love the story. They ask for it by name, the way children ask for the stories that give them just the right amount to be afraid of.

He checks his locks every night. Twice. His children have asked him about this. He has told them it is just a habit. This is the only lie he tells them, and he tells it because they are young enough to believe the world has edges that hold, and he intends for them to believe this for as long as possible, because he knows exactly how long it lasts.

He never tells them about Mr. Darnell. Mr. Darnell sat in the covered walkway of the Tillman Arms every afternoon until the building was shuttered. He played checkers with Calvin when Calvin's knees allowed, and when they didn't he sat alone with the board. He said to anyone who would listen that he had known the moment he saw her cross the parking lot. That the only thing he wished was that he had moved sooner.

Darnell Webb died at eighty-one years old in the spring of the year the Tillman Arms was shuttered. Calvin Priest gave the eulogy. He said that Darnell had been his opponent in thirty years of checkers and had beaten him more times than he could count and had been a good man who carried something heavy for a long time without letting it bend him. He said Darnell had told him, near the end, that he felt like he was the last one watching and that he didn't know who was going to watch after him.

He never tells his children that somewhere in the world, in all likelihood, there is still an unlocked door.

*— end of act three —*

# Coda

*And my soul from out that shadow that lies floating on the floor*
*Shall be lifted — nevermore.*
— Edgar Allan Poe, "The Raven"

I have found Orson Baer. I know what city he is in. I know the neighborhood. I know the building. I have looked at the building on the street map the way I looked at the fourth floor of the Benjamin Hooks Library on a Tuesday evening years ago, before I knew what I was looking at.

I have decided not to contact him.

I have thought about this decision the way I think through problems in my professional life — working through the failure modes, identifying the unintended consequences, distinguishing between what a system is designed to do and what it actually does when you set it in motion. What would I say. What would he do with what I said. Whether knowing changes anything, or whether knowing only means that you carry what he is already carrying with the additional weight of a stranger's confirmation.

I decided it would not help him.

And there is the other thing. The thing that took me longer to say plainly to myself.

I have a son. He has a wife. They have a child. I know what kind of house they keep — I have been in that house, I have sat at that table, I have looked at the drawing on their refrigerator held up by a magnet from somewhere they visited that meant something to them. I know what kind of house they keep the way I know what kind of house Henrik Bär kept and Edmund Behr kept and Marcus Baer kept, because I know what to look for now and I can see it in my own son's house as clearly as I can see it in a Bavarian church record or a Quitman County deed.

Contacting Orson means putting myself in the story. It means the genealogist who found the thread is now attached to the thread, and the thread has a new household attached to it, and she follows the thread. She has always followed the thread. Across an ocean and a hundred and sixty years and the full width of American history, the thread continues and she follows it, and I am not willing to be the one who gives her a new direction to follow.

So I do not contact him. I write this book instead. I put the warning into the world in the only form I have available, and I let the world carry it to whoever needs it, and I do not make myself visible in the carrying.

Oskar checked the treeline on the mill road every afternoon for the rest of his life.

Ezra watched the cotton fields from his cane-bottomed chair until the spring morning he didn't get up.

Darnell Webb sat in the covered walkway of the Tillman Arms until the building was shuttered, watching the parking lot, waiting for something he could not name and could not stop.

I write it down. I sign my name. I go home and I check my locks.

The rest is yours to carry.

Lock your door tonight.

It probably won't be enough.

But lock it anyway.

*—J.G.*

*Hernando, Mississippi*

# Acknowledgements

This book, my first attempt at horror fiction, owes a particular debt to Anne Rice, whose *Interview with the Vampire* first showed me that the most frightening thing a writer can do is tell the truth in a steady voice and let the reader decide what to believe. I have tried to do that here. Whether I have succeeded is yours to judge.

It owes an equal or greater debt to Mrs. Sylvia Bond, who taught English at Harding Academy in Memphis in the 1970's and 80's, and who insisted that good writing has a shape. The shape she gave me was the five-paragraph theme: introduction, three body paragraphs, conclusion. I have used it ever since, in engineering reports and magazine articles and, it turns out, in whatever this book is. Setup (thesis statement?), three acts, coda. Mrs. Bond's structure, wearing strange clothes that would not have surprised her coming from me. I hope she would recognize it. I hope she would approve.

My wife Mary has listened to me talk non-stop about this story since the idea first popped into my head. She never asked me to stop. That is its own kind of courage.

## About the Author

Jeff Gatlin has lived in and around Memphis, Tennessee, and north Mississippi his entire life. He has been an amateur genealogist for more than three decades, which means he has much of his life in close proximity to the kind of history that does not appear in textbooks — the history that survives in courthouse deed books and church records and the memories of old people who choose their words carefully when strangers ask questions.

He has been a student of that history since elementary school, when the *World Book Encyclopedia* occupied more of his attention than he really had time for. As an amateur genealogist in adulthood, following family lines through ship manifests and census records and the silences that appear in documents when something has happened that the surviving community preferred not to write down. He has learned to read those silences as carefully as the words.

He kept offices in the Binghamton neighborhood of Memphis for twenty years after spending his very early years at the eastern edge of that same neighborhood.

He lives in Hernando, Mississippi with his wife Mary.

www.ingramcontent.com/pod-product-compliance
Lightning Source LLC
LaVergne TN
LVHW090538110826
845146LV00003B/1156

* 9 7 9 8 9 9 5 2 2 9 9 2 6 *